All About Me

Things I Do

By Meg Gaertner

level 1 little blue readers

www.littlebluehousebooks.com

Little Blue House is distributed by North Star Editions:
sales@northstareditions.com | 888-417-0195

Produced for Little Blue House by Red Line Editorial.

Photographs ©: bowdenimages/iStockphoto, cover; Wavebreakmedia/iStockphoto, 4, 12–13; FatCamera/iStockphoto, 7, 8–9; Hasnuddin/Shutterstock Images, 11; mvaligursky/iStockphoto, 15; slobo/iStockphoto, 16 (top left); tiler84/iStockphoto, 16 (top right); MmeEmil/iStockphoto, 16 (bottom left); Alexander Tolstykh/Shutterstock Images, 16 (bottom right)

Library of Congress Control Number: 2019908256

ISBN
978-1-64619-004-1 (hardcover)
978-1-64619-043-0 (paperback)
978-1-64619-082-9 (ebook pdf)
978-1-64619-121-5 (hosted ebook)

Printed in the United States of America
Mankato, MN
012020

About the Author

Meg Gaertner enjoys reading, writing, dancing, and being outside. She lives in Minnesota.

Table of Contents

piano

Things I Do

I play music.

I play the piano.

I play a sport.

I play basketball.

I play in the gym.

basketball

I read a book.

I read with friends.

I turn the pages.

book

I draw a picture.

I draw a tree.

I use crayons.

picture

I bake with my dad.

I bake cookies.

I can't wait to eat them.

dad
cookies

I play outside.

I play with my dog.

I run in the grass.